A HOME FOR ERNIE

by Amy Reichert

Illustrated by Virginia Bishop Tawresey

ISBN 1-880812-11-8

Published by Storytellers Ink

Printed in the United States of America

Dedication

To Richard and Nat with love.

And to Bert and Ernie, and Harley
and Diva–my furry friends who help
make our house a home.

Other Books by Storytellers Ink

A Bug C
Beautiful Joe
Black Beauty
Bustop the Cat and Mrs. Lin
Cousin Charlie the Crow
Father Goose & His Goslings
If a Seahorse Wore a Saddle
I Thought I Heard a Tiger Roar
J.G. Cougar's Great Adventure
Jonathan Jasper Jeremy Jones
Kitty the Raccoon
Little Annie of Christian Creek
Lobo the Wolf
Not For Sadie
Redruff the Partridge of Don Valley
Sandy of Laguna
Sully the Seal and Alley the Cat
The Blue Kangaroo
The Blue Kangaroo at the Zoo
The Butterfly Garden
The Living Mountain
The Lost and Found Puppy
The Pacing Mustang
Tweak and the Absolutely Right Whale
William's Story

Contents

Chapter I

The Pet Shop

Two little faces peered into the pet shop window.

Ernie sat in his cage on the other side, staring back.

"Look how cute that puppy is," exclaimed the little boy.

"And cuddly," sighed his baby sister. "I bet he'd fit just perfectly in my arms."

"Oh, please Mom, Dad, can't we buy him?" they pleaded.

"I'm afraid not," said their father. "You two aren't old enough yet to take care of a dog."

"Then let's get him for you, Mom, for your birthday," suggested the little boy. "You must be old enough to take care of a dog by now."

"Oh, I'm old enough, all right," she laughed. "Old enough to know that a puppy needs to be walked and fed and brushed every day, and that it needs to be trained to behave and not wet the floor. Having a puppy is a lot like having another baby. And for now your Dad and I have enough to do with two little children. We really don't need any more."

"But I'll walk him with my dolly," said the little girl.

"And I'll feed him all my vegetables," added the boy, "so he'll grow big and tall like me."

"That's exactly what he's going to do," said their father. "Only a lot bigger and a lot faster than you two might think. I'm afraid you won't think this puppy is so cute and cuddly when he doesn't fit in your arms anymore. I'm not so sure you'll want to play with him then."

"We'll play with him!" cried the children. "We promise."

"Maybe we can get a dog next year," said their mother, "when we move into a bigger house with a bigger backyard. You'll both be a little older then, and a dog would be a lot happier with more room to run around."

"Good idea," said their father, as he gently pulled the children away from the pet shop window. "Let's think about getting a dog next year when we can give it a really good home."

The rest of the family moved down the street, but the little boy lingered behind. He took one long, last look at Ernie. "I wish I could take you with me," he said sadly. "But don't worry little puppy, I'm sure you'll find a good home soon."

Chapter II
The Dog Show

Early the next morning a dog trainer came into the pet shop.
He didn't care that Ernie was cute and cuddly, or that it felt nice to hold him in his arms. He looked at his teeth, his eyes and his coat. And then he bought him for one reason, and one reason only.

"Ernie," he said, "I'm tired of training carpet wetters, slipper chewers and dogs who bite the mail carrier's knees. I want to train a dog I can be proud of— a show dog who will win silky blue ribbons and big gold trophies. I want a champion. Nothing more and nothing less will do."

So the trainer took Ernie home and for a while nobody expected much of anything from him. After all, he was still just a young and playful pup.

But soon he began to grow up...and up...and up...until one day the

trainer said, "You're getting mighty big, Ernie. Soon you'll be a full grown dog. We'd better start your training. It's certainly not too early–not if you're going to be a champ."

That very afternoon Ernie's lessons began. Day after day, week after week, he trained in a big, empty field, practicing over and over again all the important things a champion needs to know.

"Heel, Ernie, heel," the trainer would call, and Ernie would walk obediently by his side.

"Sit! Good dog. Now stay! Staaay! Okay, now... come! Good dog!"

Ernie would beam with pride. All his hard work in the hot dusty field was for one reason, and one reason only. It wasn't ribbons or trophies that Ernie worked for–it was to make his owner happy and proud.

At last the day of Ernie's first dog show arrived. All morning long people streamed into a big green meadow. They brought picnic baskets and checkered table cloths, kickballs and kites. Old and young people came, dog lovers and fun lovers. They laughed and chatted and ate and played until it was time for the show to begin.

The most beautiful dogs from around the county were gathered in the center ring. They were all so quiet and well behaved. All of them, that is, except Ernie.

Ernie panted with excitement. He squirmed with delight. He wanted to race around and meet everyone there.

But his trainer had other ideas.

YANK! went the chain around Ernie's neck. "Be still and stand up straight," he hissed. "Remember, this is a dog show–not a party!"

Ernie remembered. For the rest of the show he stood quietly, watching the other dogs perform.

Finally it was Ernie's turn.

"Fetch!" ordered the judge. "Drop!...Sit!...Stand!"

Ernie was magnificent.

The crowd went wild.

"What a champ!" someone cried.

"What a star!" said another.

"Bravo to the winner," they shouted. "Bravo Ernie, bravo!"

But the show wasn't over yet. It was time for the judge's inspection.

"This is the most important part of the competition," the trainer reminded Ernie. "So please behave yourself. No jumping. No licking. No wagging your tail. Just do what you're told–nothing else!"

The judge bent down to inspect Ernie's coat.

"Beautiful condition," he murmured. Ernie stood still as a stone.

"Well-shaped eyes," he told the crowd. Ernie didn't bat a lash.

"Perfect teeth," he congratulated the owner. Ernie didn't dare even swallow.

"A truly remarkable dog!" cried the judge. Then he smiled—his first smile of the day.

The trainer beamed with delight, and the crowd roared with applause.

Ernie was so happy that everybody liked him that he jumped up on his back legs, threw his paws around the judge's neck and gave him a big, long, wet, sloppy lick. The kind that means, "I think you're pretty terrific too!"

"Oh my!" sniffed the judge.

"Oh dear!" gasped the crowd.

The trainer was too shocked to speak.

But no one was surprised later when Ernie came in last, and when a beautiful poodle won the show.

That evening the trainer told Ernie, "Your days as a show dog are over." He picked up the pet section of the want ads. "I'm going to have to find you a new home."

And in no time at all, he did.

Chapter III
Life On the Farm

The very next day Ernie was sold to a farmer. The farmer didn't buy him because he was cute and cuddly, or because it felt so nice to hold him in his arms. He bought him for one reason and one reason only.

"Ernie," he said, "I live on a big farm and I'm getting too old and too tired to do all the chores by myself. I need help. I need a good farm dog. Nothing more and nothing less will do."

As soon as they arrived the farmer took Ernie on a tour of his farm.

"These are my cows," he said pointing to a small herd grazing in the pasture. "Their milk is rich and smooth and creamy. And they are as gentle and sweet as they are big."

Ernie looked up at their huge bodies and suddenly felt very small.

"Mooooo," said one loudly and Ernie jumped. The farmer laughed but quickly moved on.

Next to the pasture was a pen full of pigs. Some were napping in the sun. Some were sunning on their backs, and others were rooting around for tidbits to eat.

"These are my prize winning pigs," said the farmer. "They come in first every year at the fair."

Next to the pig pen was a yard full of chickens. They all rushed up to the farmer, clucking and clacking their sharp beaks at once.

"You can't find better egg-laying hens than these," said the farmer. He reached into the grain bin and tossed them a handful of corn. The chickens scurried after the food as fast as they could. The yard erupted into a cloud of bright feathers.

What excitement! What fun! Ernie liked these birds. He liked the farm. He liked the farmer. He liked the pigs. He even liked the cows. And he just knew that as soon as he found out what he was supposed to do, he'd like being a farm dog too.

"Ernie," said the farmer, "all my animals have jobs. The cows make milk. The chickens lay eggs. And the pigs eat a lot so they'll grow up nice and big. But you, Ernie, will have the most important job of all. As farm dog it will be your job to get all the animals where they need to be so they can do their jobs well."

He pointed to a cluster of buildings.

"The cows sleep over in that shed so they're ready for milking first thing in the morning."

"The pigs sleep in the barn where it's safe and cozy and warm."

"And the chickens spend their nights in the coop where they can rest quietly and lay their eggs."

The farmer turned to Ernie. "It's not easy herding all these animals in and out, day after day. Do you think you can help me, Ernie?"

Ernie barked excitedly. He would try his very best.

The next morning Ernie woke up early, eager to start work. As soon as the farmer opened the door, Ernie burst out and raced off ahead. He ran up to the cows in the shed, and over to the pigs in the barn, and around to the chickens in the coop, barking and jumping with good morning cheer.

One of the cows got nervous and kicked open the door. A piglet, wondering what all the noise was about, wiggled through a loose board in the barn to see. A mischievous chicken pecked his way out of the coop hoping for some adventure and fun. It wasn't long before all the animals were running around free, and Ernie was dashing madly behind.

He chased the cows up a hill and the pigs through a meadow and the chickens deep into the woods. It took the farmer all that day to put things right, and still two chickens were stuck in a tree.

That night the farmer's wife said to her husband, "Homer, we had better get rid of that dog. We won't have any milk, pork, or eggs if he stays another day."

The farmer liked Ernie, but he knew his wife was right.

"Ernie," said the farmer, "you're a good dog, but you're no farm dog, and so I'm afraid that you just can't stay. But don't worry, I'll find you a good home."

And in no time at all he did...or so he thought.

Chapter IV

Guarding the Grounds

Ernie's new home was big and beautiful, surrounded by gardens and protected by a high stone wall. His new owner was very rich. She didn't buy Ernie because he was cute and cuddly, or because it felt so nice to hold him in her arms. She bought him for one reason and one reason only.

"Ernie," she said, "I dislike dogs, but I hate thieves even more! They want all my diamonds and gold and jewels. Well, they're not going to get my treasures," she said. "That's why I bought you. I want a dog who will act fierce and mean and scare all the burglars away."

"Ernie," she said, "what I need is a good watchdog. Nothing more and nothing less will do."

She showed Ernie around the grounds and ordered him to bark and growl if anyone came near. "You'll be on duty around the clock," she said. "Twenty-four hours a day. You won't be allowed inside the house or taken on walks. Just do your job and obey."

And Ernie did. But he was terribly sad and lonely. He didn't have a single friend. His new owner didn't like him. The servants had no time for him. And strangers kept their distance, thinking he was ferocious and mean.

Late one night, when everyone was out, a big bone came sailing over the wall. Ernie ran to investigate.

He heard a loud thump nearby. And then another. Two masked men had jumped over the wall and were standing in the shadows beside him.

Ernie assumed they had come for their bone and quickly ran to retrieve it.

"Good dog," said one of the men as Ernie brought the bone to him.

"You can have it," said the other. "We brought it especially for you."

Ernie was overjoyed. It was the first treat he'd had since becoming a watch dog and the first kindness that anyone had shown him. If more friendly visitors would bring him bones at night, thought Ernie, then maybe his job wouldn't be so bad after all.

The masked men tip-toed quietly around the house.

They found a half-open window and climbed in. Ernie was too busy with his bone to notice.

The men went through the house with sacks slung over their backs.
One headed for the dining room and started filling his sack with silver bowls,
candlesticks and trays.

The other went straight to the owner's bedroom, where he found drawers full of glittering jewels. He grabbed necklaces, bracelets, rings and pearls, and emptied them all into his black sack.

The thieves didn't stop until their sacks were stuffed and they couldn't carry anymore.

Before leaving, one of the men gave Ernie a pat on the back and said, "You're a good dog, you deserved that bone." Ernie was sorry to see his new friends go and hoped they would return to see him soon.

When his owner came home and discovered all her treasures were gone, she was furious. She stormed through the house screaming, "Where is that dog?" and found him soundly asleep with his bone.

"Useless creature!" she shrieked. "You're no watchdog," she moaned. "You let thieves take all of my beautiful things! Out!" she yelled. "Get out of my sight! First thing tomorrow I'm going to get rid of you!"

And she did. She called the animal shelter to take him away.

Chapter V
No Place To Call Home

The shelter was the saddest place Ernie had ever been. It was filled with animals that no one wanted.

ERNIE
AGE 1½
Golden Retriever

There were animals that cost too much to feed and animals with too many young. There were fighters and yappers and scratchers and shedders. There were runaways that no one bothered to claim.

Some were cute. Some weren't so cute. Some were pure-bred. And some were mutts.

But there was one thing that all of them shared. They were all unwanted. No one in the world loved any of them enough to give them a permanent home.

Ernie was no different. And as the days passed and nobody came for him, he began to lose hope.

After all, he told himself, he had failed as a show dog, as a farm dog and as a watchdog. What use was he to anyone, anyway? Maybe he would never have a home again.

Then one day the shelter manager showed a family through the kennels.

They stopped in front of a cage full of puppies.

"This one's awfully cute," said the mother, pointing to a fluffy white poodle.

"This is a nice one," said the father, scratching a little Pekinese under the chin.

"What do you think, kids?" he asked. "Do you like either one of these?"

The boy shrugged. "Yeah, I guess so, but could we look at some more?" He started walking down an aisle of cages, looking carefully into each and every one.

"I'll know our dog when I see him," the boy thought to himself. "And he'll be the best dog that ever was."

Ernie was so excited when he saw the little boy coming that he did everything he had been taught not to do.

He jumped up and down, ran around the cage, and barked and howled to get the boy's attention.

The trainer would have been cross with him, the farmer upset, and the woman disgusted.

But the boy just stopped. Then he smiled and ran over to Ernie's cage.

Ernie whined with joy and licked the boy's face a dozen times through the bars. The boy petted Ernie's nose and laughed.

"I've found him. I've found our dog!" he shouted. His family came running from all directions to see.

"He's so gentle," said his sister when Ernie nuzzled her hand with his nose. "I like him!"

The boy turned eagerly to his parents.

"But I thought you kids wanted a puppy," said the father, laughing. "This is a grown dog."

"That's right," said their mother. "He's far too big to hold in your arms."

The little boy looked long and hard at Ernie. "I think he's perfect just the way he is," he whispered. "He's the one we want. He's the dog for us."

He looked at his sister who was petting Ernie through the cage. She nodded eagerly.

Chapter VI
Home at Last

So Ernie went home with his new family. They didn't want a show dog, or a farm dog, or a guard dog. They just wanted a companion and friend – nothing more and nothing less.

And Ernie finally had what he wanted too, people to love, and people who loved him in return—nothing more and nothing less.